First published in the USA in 2019 by Cassava Republic Press

Abuja - London

Designed and typeset by Al's Fingers

ISBN: 978-1-911115-68-7

A CIP catalogue record for this book is available from the British Library.

Printed and bound in the UK by Bell & Bain Ltd.

www.cassavarepublic.biz

MYLO FREEMAN

Hair, it's a Family Affair!

"Quiet children!" Miss Brown, the teacher, claps her hands.
"It's Macy's turn to tell us about her family."
Macy's eyes light up. "I'm going to tell you all about
my family's hair!"

"When my grandma was young, she had a **big Afro** like a ball of cotton candy," says Macy. "She looked really amazing. Her Afro is smaller now, but she still looks amazing."

"My big sister and her friends have different hairstyles: cornrows, locks and an Afro. They **think** they look **really cool**," Macy chuckles.

"My mom has promised my little brother **a cute new haircut.** I hope he can keep still!" says Macy.

"I love combing my baby sister's hair," Macy smiles.

"She has the softest, sweetest-smelling hair and I'm the only one she lets brush it."

"My mom always says that
hair is a family affair!
And helping each other saves a
lot of time too!" Macy giggles.

"I love my big cousin Kiki.
One week her hair is purple and the
next it's bright pink!"

"She has so much **style**." Macy sighs.
"I want to look like her when I grow up."

"When I grow up, I'm going to be a famous doctor and **my best friend Troy** will be a famous hairdresser."

"Well, now I have talked about everyone in **my family** and their hair, except for one person…" Macy pauses.

"And that's my dad, because he has no hair at all!"
Macy chuckles. "But we love him anyway!"

All the children in the classroom clap
and cheer.

"Well done, Macy! That was lovely,"
says Miss Brown.

More from Mylo Freeman, author of the *Princess Arabella* series:

Princess Arabella's Birthday

Ruby-encrusted roller skates, a golden bicycle, a cuddly mouse, a tea set, a doll's pram? No, Princess Arabella wants something different for her birthday: an elephant.

But will she get what she wants?

ISBN 978-1911115373

Princess Arabella and the Giant Cake

It is almost Granny's birthday and Princess Arabella and her friends set out to bake the most DELICIOUS and most GIGANTIC cake in the entire world. But who will be the winner – Princess Arabella, Prince Mimoun, Princess Sophie or Princess Ling? And what is that surprise in the Giant Cake?!

ISBN 978-1911115663

Princess Arabella Mixes Colors

Princess Arabella thinks her room is boring. So she decides she's going to do something about that – all by herself. She mixes up some paint and in no time at all her room looks fabulous.

A delightful picture book with fun information about mixing colors.

ISBN 978-1911115366

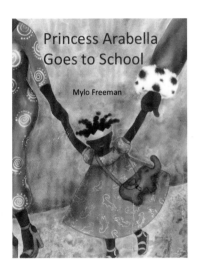

Princess Arabella Goes to School

Princess Arabella and her friends embark upon their first day at Princess School. They find themselves taking some very unusual lessons – and when they are allowed to bring their pets to school, fun and games ensue!

ISBN 978-1911115656

Every Girl is a Princess

In this book, you'll meet princesses from all over the world. They all have their favorite animal and their own crown. But who fits the remaining crown?

A cheerful and colorful picture book that shows that a little princess (or prince) hides in every child.

ISBN 978-1911115380